In the Spotlight

Adapted by Mary Man-Kong
Based on the original screenplay by Alison Taylor
Illustrated by Ulkutay Design Group

Special thanks to Diane Reichenberger, Cindy Ledermann, Ann McNeill, Kim Culmone, Emily Kelly, Sharon Woloszyk, Carla Alford, Rita Lichtwardt, Kathy Berry, Rob Hudnut, David Wiebe, Shelley Dvi-Vardhana, Gabrielle Miles, Technicolor, and Walter P. Martishius.

A Random House PICTUREBACK® Book

Random House 🏠 New York

Published in the United States by Random House Children's Books, a division of Random House, Inc.,
1745 Broadway, New York, NY 10019, and in Canada by Random House of Canada Limited, Toronto.
No part of this book may be reproduced or copied in any form without permission from the copyright owner.
Pictureback, Random House, and the Random House colophon are registered trademarks of Random House, Inc.
ISBN: 978-0-307-98106-6
randomhouse.com/kids   Printed in the United States of America   10 9 8 7 6 5 4 3 2 1

It was the day of the big ballet recital and everyone was excited—especially Kristyn. The young dancer loved all the spins, jumps, and twirls in all the famous ballets.

Kristyn watched the star ballerina, Tara, rehearse. She wished that she could dance the lead role.

When it was Kristyn's turn to dance, she glided and twirled beautifully on the stage—and then she started to add some of her own dance moves.

"Stop!" cried her strict dance teacher, Madame Natasha. "I've seen other girls attempt to dance their own ideas, and I promise you, the story does not end well."

"I just get caught up in the music," Kristyn said dreamily. "And my feet do their own thing."

After rehearsal, Kristyn noticed that her ballet shoe was ripped. She went with her best friend, Hailey, to see the costume designer, Madame Katerina. Hailey was Madame Katerina's assistant.

Madame Katerina searched everywhere. She handed Kristyn a pair of pink shoes. "These are for you, my dear," she said.

Kristyn sat down and slowly laced up the pink ballet shoes. As she stood up, the shoes began to glitter and sparkle. Magically, Kristyn's dress transformed into a beautiful blue-and-pink tutu and her hair turned strawberry blond. The costume shop had disappeared—and Kristyn and Hailey found themselves in a strange forest!

Two handsome young men named Albrecht and Hilarion approached Kristyn and asked her to dance. Kristyn soon realized that the men thought she was Giselle from the ballet *Giselle*. Kristyn was thrilled! She danced the classic steps perfectly, then added her own unique, graceful steps to the ballet.

Kristyn had never felt more alive. "I love these shoes!" she exclaimed.

After the dance, Hilarion and Albrecht started to argue about who should marry Giselle. Not wanting any trouble, Hailey quickly pulled Kristyn into the forest.

Suddenly, a grand ice sleigh appeared. "What is happening here?" the evil Snow Queen demanded. "I will not tolerate this kind of disruption. The ballet must be perfect. Bring the girl to me!"

As the girls ran through the forest, Hailey realized what was happening. "It must be the shoes," said Hailey. "When you put them on, we ended up in the middle of the ballet. But if you take them off . . ."

"No way," said Kristyn. She had never been the star ballerina before this.

Just then, Kristyn's hair turned a rich chestnut brown and her dress transformed into a gorgeous purple gown. A group of ballet dancers appeared and placed a glittering swan crown on her head. Kristyn had become the Swan Queen Odette in the ballet *Swan Lake*!

A handsome young prince named Siegfried appeared and asked Kristyn to dance. As they performed a beautiful duet, the prince couldn't take his eyes off Kristyn.

"I know we've just met," said the prince, "but I want to invite you to a party tonight at my royal pavilion." Kristyn graciously accepted.

After the prince left, the girls noticed a man in a dark cloak approaching. They quickly recognized him as the evil magician Rothbart from *Swan Lake*. Rothbart wanted the prince to marry his daughter Odile, so he magically made her look like Odette. Then he cast an evil spell on Kristyn and Hailey—transforming them into swans! Every day when the sun set, they would change back into humans. But when the sun rose, the girls would change back into swans!

Kristyn knew from the ballet that the only way to break the spell was to make the prince fall in love with her. She and Hailey flew as fast as they could and reached the palace just at sunset. When the prince saw Odile and Kristyn, he didn't know who the real Odette was. Kristyn had an idea. She started to dance, and the prince recognized her graceful, unique moves. He chose Kristyn and the spell was broken!

Unfortunately, the Snow Queen had witnessed the change in the *Swan Lake* ballet—and kidnapped Hailey!

Kristyn quickly raced to the Queen's palace, where she found Hailey frozen in a block of ice. The evil Snow Queen cast a spell on Kristyn, controlling every move she made. But Kristyn closed her eyes and concentrated. She began to spin and dance in her own beautiful style.

"Stop that!" cried the Queen. "There is only one way to tell the story."

"No," Kristyn replied. "There is more than one way."

As she uttered those words, rays of light shone through the palace. The spell was broken—and the Snow Queen disappeared forever.

The ice around Hailey melted, setting her free. Kristyn hurried over to her best friend and gave her a big hug.

"Let's go home," Kristyn said.

As the young dancer untied her pink shoes, the ice palace began to fade away. Before they knew it, the two friends were safely back at their ballet school.

There was no time to waste! The recital was about to begin, and ballet scouts were in the audience. The scouts would be choosing dancers for an international ballet company.

When it was Kristyn's turn to dance, she glided onto the stage. The music seemed to flow into Kristyn, and she performed her own unique dance moves with all her heart. As she twirled, her dress transformed into a pink gown and her hair flowed beautifully behind her. Everyone was amazed! Even Madame Katerina nodded approvingly.

After the recital, the ballet scouts chose Tara to star in their production of *Giselle*. But they also chose Kristyn and her original dance style as the inspiration for a new ballet.

Kristyn and Hailey were so happy. Kristyn had followed her heart and her ballet dreams had come true.